You Know It!

SAMMY
the Steiger

Gotcha!

FRANKIE
the Farmall

Got It!

CODY
the Combine

Hey Dudes!

BAILEY
the Baler

Go Team!

KELLIE
the Combine

Awesome!

PETER
the Patriot Sprayer

VROOM!

SCOOTER
the CIH Scout

Let's Do It!

TAMMI
the Tiller

Details!

EVAN
the Early Riser Planter

This book belongs to:

Name: _ _ _ _ _ _ _ _ _ _ _ _ _ _ _ _ _ _

Favorite color: _ _ _ _ _ _ _ _ _ _ _ _ _

Big Tractors
with Casey & Friends

Hi! I'm Casey, and this is my friend, Tillus. Welcome to Happy Skies Farm!

Casey has a busy day ahead, and she needs her tractors to help. Let's go!

Happy Skies Farm

Farming Takes a Team!

Farming is a lot of hard work. Each day brings new challenges. I don't worry — my team helps me get every job done!

Wow! Look at all the things we do!

The Muscles of Happy Skies Farm

I have many tractors, and each one helps me in different ways. Big Red the Magnum and Sammy Steiger are my biggest tractors. They are too large to work in tight spaces around the farmyard. Can you guess what their job is?

We are the "muscles" on Happy Skies Farm! Casey relies on us to work the fields.

TILLUS TALK

Size Matters!

Big Red and Sammy's size helps them work the toughest jobs on the farm.

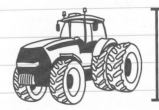

11ft.

Big Red stands 11 feet tall—that's like stacking 15 of these books end to end! And he weighs more than 22 cows combined.

x44

Sammy is as tall as 17 books stacked end to end—about 13 feet. And he weighs more than 44 cows combined.

Whew! That's a lot!

5

Farming Flashback

Before tractors were invented, farmers used horses to pull equipment. The number of horses used for a job depended on how much power was needed to do it.

It took 4 horses to complete that job!

Horsepower!

The invention of the engine changed farming forever!

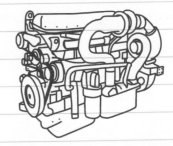

Engine power is measured in horsepower (hp)!

$$1hp = $$

Side Note!

Vehicles like tractors, cars, planes, and boats have engines that are measured in horsepower.

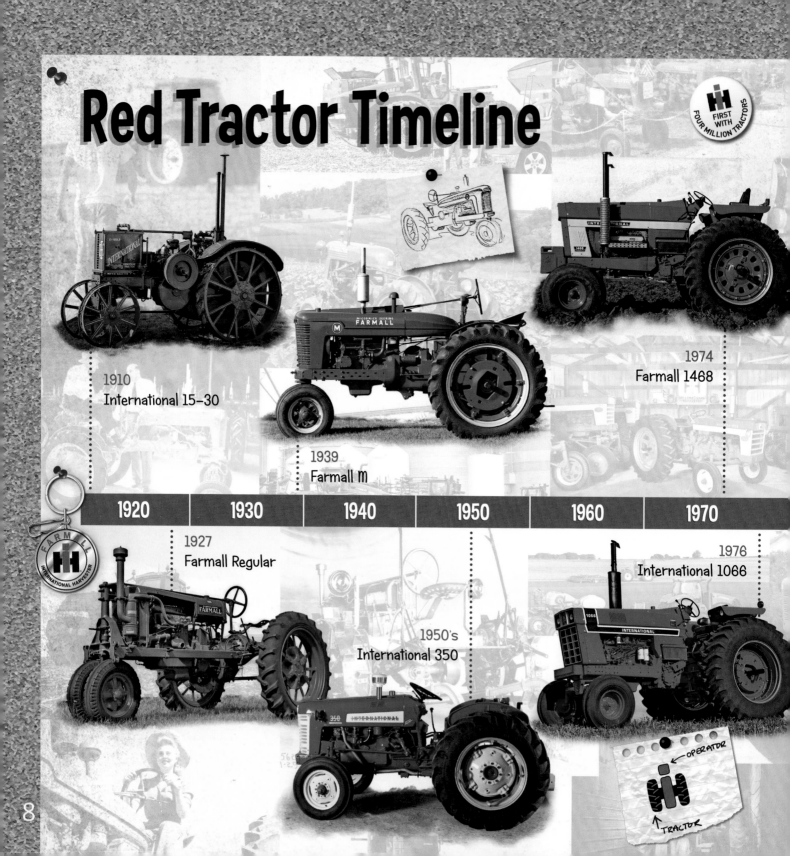

Red Tractor Timeline

FIRST WITH FOUR MILLION TRACTORS

1910
International 15-30

1939
Farmall M

1974
Farmall 1468

| 1920 | 1930 | 1940 | 1950 | 1960 | 1970 |

1927
Farmall Regular

1950's
International 350

1976
International 1066

OPERATOR

TRACTOR

1991
Magnum 7120

2006
Steiger STX 380

????
Steiger _____

1980 | 1990 | 2000 | 2010 | ????

1984
International 5288

2014
Steiger 620

Over the years, tractors have grown in size and power! How do you think tractors will change in the future?

CASE IH COUNTRY
BE READY.

CASE IH
AGRICULTURE

9

Pulling Power

A lot of farm equipment does not have an engine, so it cannot move by itself. I depend on Big Red and Sammy's super strength to pull it.

Thanks to my large engine, I have the power to pull Tammi.

Only the strongest tractors can pull me!

Tractors Work Out with Weights!

Sometimes tractors need special weights when they work.

When a tractor pulls heavy equipment, the extra weight can cause the front of the tractor to lift off the ground.

Farmers put weights on the front of their tractors. The added weight in front keeps the tractor safely on the ground while it pulls the equipment.

Pulling Power in the Fields

Big Red pulls me so I can till the soil and get it ready for planting crops. Let's get moving, Big Red!

I pull the wagon while Kellie unloads wheat. Harvesting is heaps of fun!

Big Red pulls me as I plant seeds into the soil. He goes the right speed, so I don't miss any seeds!

Power to Make Machines Work

Some pieces of farm equipment, called implements, have parts that need extra power to make them work. Big Red and Sammy supply the power to make parts move!

Sammy gives me liquid power to carefully plant each seed in the soil.

Big Red gives me spinning power to turn loose hay into nice tight bales.

TILLUS TALK

Hooking up to the Power Outlet!

Tractors have special tools that transfer power from their engine to the implement.

Liquid Power!

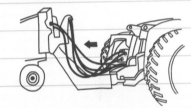

Evan uses hydraulic power. That's power created when liquid moves through hoses between Evan and Sammy.

Spinning Power!

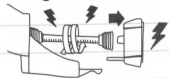

Bailey connects to a tool on the back of Big Red, called power takeoff or PTO. The PTO spins, creating power for Bailey.

15

The Wonder of Wheels and Duals

Tractors like Big Red are very heavy. So what keeps them from sinking into the soft soil? It's their wheels, of course!

My wheels are extra large and wide. Their size spreads my weight evenly over the soil. That keeps me from sinking in the fields.

TILLUS TALK

Duals Are Double the Fun!

Big Red has two wheels on each back axle. They are called duals.

Duals help Big Red float over soft soil. That's because the extra tire spreads his weight over a larger area.

17

Making Tracks

At certain times of the year, the soil is wet and very soft. Heavy tractors like Sammy can easily sink in the fields — causing a lot of problems. Yikes! But don't worry. Sammy won't get stuck!

TILLUS TALK

More Traction, Less Compaction!

Sammy's tracks are designed to keep the soil soft like a sponge.

Soil that is pressed down too much becomes hard and dense like a brick.

Why does it matter? Plants grow best in soft soil!

You're right, Casey! That's because the large, flat bottom of my tracks helps me "float" over the soil. My tracks work great in dry or wet fields!

19

My Office in the Field

When it's time to plant seeds or harvest crops, I have to work long hours in the field. Some days, I sit in my tractor's cab for more than 12 hours!

STEERING »
The steering wheel controls which direction the tractor moves.

WINDSHIELD »
The windshield goes from floor to ceiling. What a view!

SEAT »
The seat is very comfortable. It can heat up when Casey's cold!

MIRRORS

The mirrors show what's happening behind the tractor.

COMPUTER

The touchscreen computer gives Casey important information.

HANDLE

The handle controls adjust speed and forward/backward motion.

ARMREST

The armrest controls operate the implement being pulled.

Precision Farming at Happy Skies Farm

Happy Skies Farm is very big, and I'm not always near my team when they work. Using Advanced Farming System (AFS) technology, I keep track of everyone no matter where they are on the farm.

The white AFS box on my roof communicates with Casey's handheld computer. She can see where we are and what we're doing at any time. AFS helps us do our jobs. It tells me where to drive when I'm in the fields.
It's amazing!

AFS works by passing information between the team's AFS boxes and satellites in space. And Casey receives the team's AFS messages through cellular signals – the same way a cell phone works. Casey receives Big Red and Sammy's information as it happens.

23

The Big Picture on Magnum

This cutaway drawing shows the inside of a Magnum. It's like looking at the tractor with X-ray glasses!

ENGINE

WEIGHTS

SIZE 'EM UP

11'0"
5'10"
6"

CAB

WHEELS

STAIRS

All that's inside of me? Awesome!

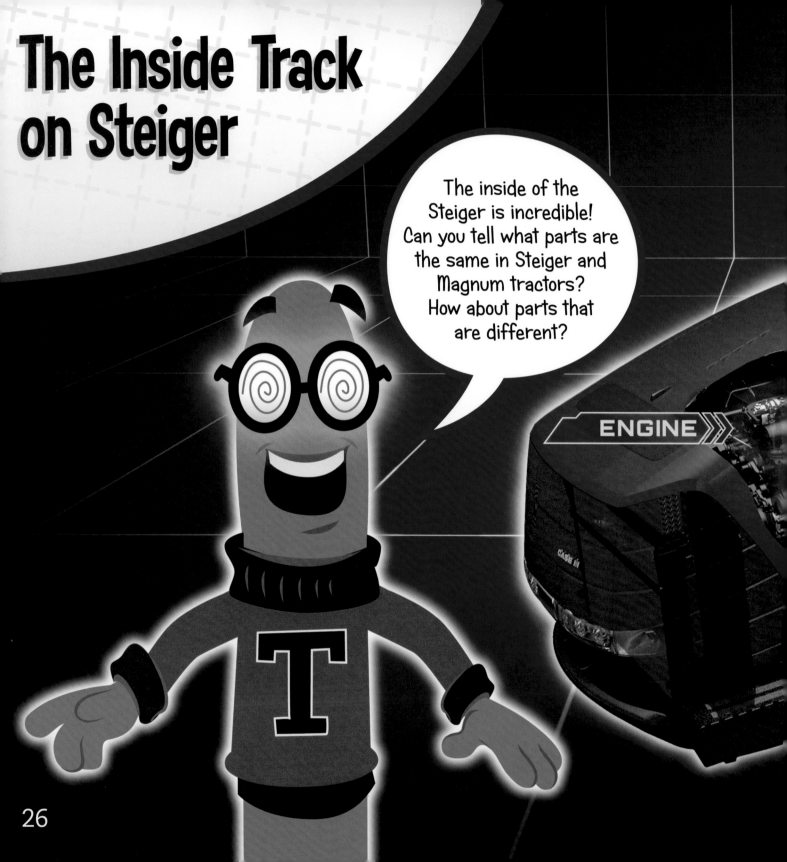

SIZE 'EM UP

13'0"

5'10"

6"

CAB

STAIRS

TRACKS

Look at all that amazing technology inside of me!

27

We Love Our Community!

Here comes Sammy. He looks great!

29

GLOSSARY

ADVANCED FARMING SYSTEM (AFS)

special technology in Case IH tractors used to help farmers do their job

AXLE

a rod that passes through a wheel to make it spin

BALES

loose hay that is pressed together and formed into squares or rolls

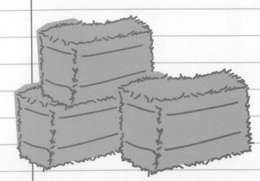

CAB

the part of the tractor where the farmer sits and works

CROPS

plants that a farmer grows

COMMUNITY

a group of people who live in the same area, such as a town or city

DUALS

two wheels that are placed on each axle of the tractor

ENGINE

a machine that turns energy into motion

HARVESTING

gathering of crops

HAY

plants grown as food for animals

HORSEPOWER

the power needed to do a certain amount of work

HYDRAULIC POWER

power created from the movement of liquid

IMPLEMENT

a machine used for farming and is pulled by a tractor

POWER

the amount of energy needed to do a certain amount of work in a period of time

POWER TAKEOFF (PTO)

spinning part on a tractor that connects with equipment to provide power

SOIL

the layer of dirt that plants grow in

TECHNOLOGY

equipment made using scientific information

TRACKS

special wheels that help to keep a tractor from sinking into the ground

TRACTOR

a powerful machine that can be driven and is used on a farm

FUN FACTS!

Tractors have lights in the front and back so they can work in the dark.

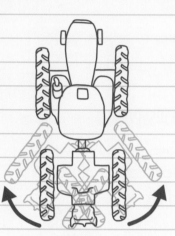

Steiger tractors are articulated, which means they can bend in the middle!

Tractors have seat belts.

Did you know that tractors are magic? They turn into fields!

The word *tractor* comes from a Latin word that means "to pull."

The first tractors were powered using steam.

Tractors are tested at the University of Nebraska. The Nebraska Test is so important that countries all over the world use the same methods to test their tractors.

Octane Press, Edition 1.0, April 1, 2015

Library of Congress Cataloging-in-Publication Data

ISBN: 1937747534 ISBN-13:978-1-937747-53-4

1. Juvenile Nonfiction—Transportation—General. 2. Juvenile Nonfiction—Lifestyles—Farm and Ranch Life.

3. Juvenile Nonfiction—Lifestyles—Country Life. 4. Juvenile Nonfiction—Concepts—Seasons

Library of Congress Control Number: 2014954291

Additional photography with permission from Lee Klancher p. 8–9;
Montgomery Design International p. 9; ThomasWerks Creative Leadership, LLC. p. 28–29;
The Wisconsin Historical Society p. 6–8 (ID7781, ID24287, ID24702, ID46590, ID27316, ID8868, ID8683, ID46668, ID42932, and ID24628)

octanepress.com

Printed in the United States

Farming keeps me busy, but I love my life!

CASEY
the Farmer

Casey depends on me for the daily weather report!

TILLUS
the Worm

Easy Peasy!

FERN
the Farmall

Be Ready!

BIG RED
the Magnum